For my parents

First published in 2013 by Child's Play (International) Ltd
Ashworth Road, Bridgemead, Swindon SN5 7YD UK

Published in USA by Child's Play Inc
250 Minot Avenue, Auburn, Maine 04210

Distributed in Australia by Child's Play Australia Pty Ltd
Unit 10/20 Narabang Way, Belrose, NSW 2085

ISBN 978-1-84643-550-8
CLP240912CPL12125508

Printed and bound in Shenzhen, China

1 3 5 7 9 10 8 6 4 2

A catalogue record of this book
is available from the British Library

www.childs-play.com

Harold
finds a voice

Courtney Dicmas

Deep in the heart of Paris,
in apartment 4B, there lived
a very clever parrot.

His name was HAROLD.

RING! RING! RING!

Harold was
a gifted bird.

burble burble burble burble

He could hear any sound just once
and copy it *perfectly.*

When Harold heard something beautiful, he simply couldn't resist the urge to repeat it.

vrrrrrmmm

VRRRMMMM!

He loved the sound
of water most.

There was only one problem.

Harold was TIRED of repeating the same old noises.

He often wondered what
other sounds were out there.

Early one morning,
Harold saw a chance
to find out...

...and took it!

Z Z Z Z Z Z Z Z

Harold couldn't believe his ears.

chop chop chop

vrrroooom

The world was full
of beautiful sounds.
Everything had
its own voice.

beep

honk

beep
beep

honk

honk

There were **BIG** voices.

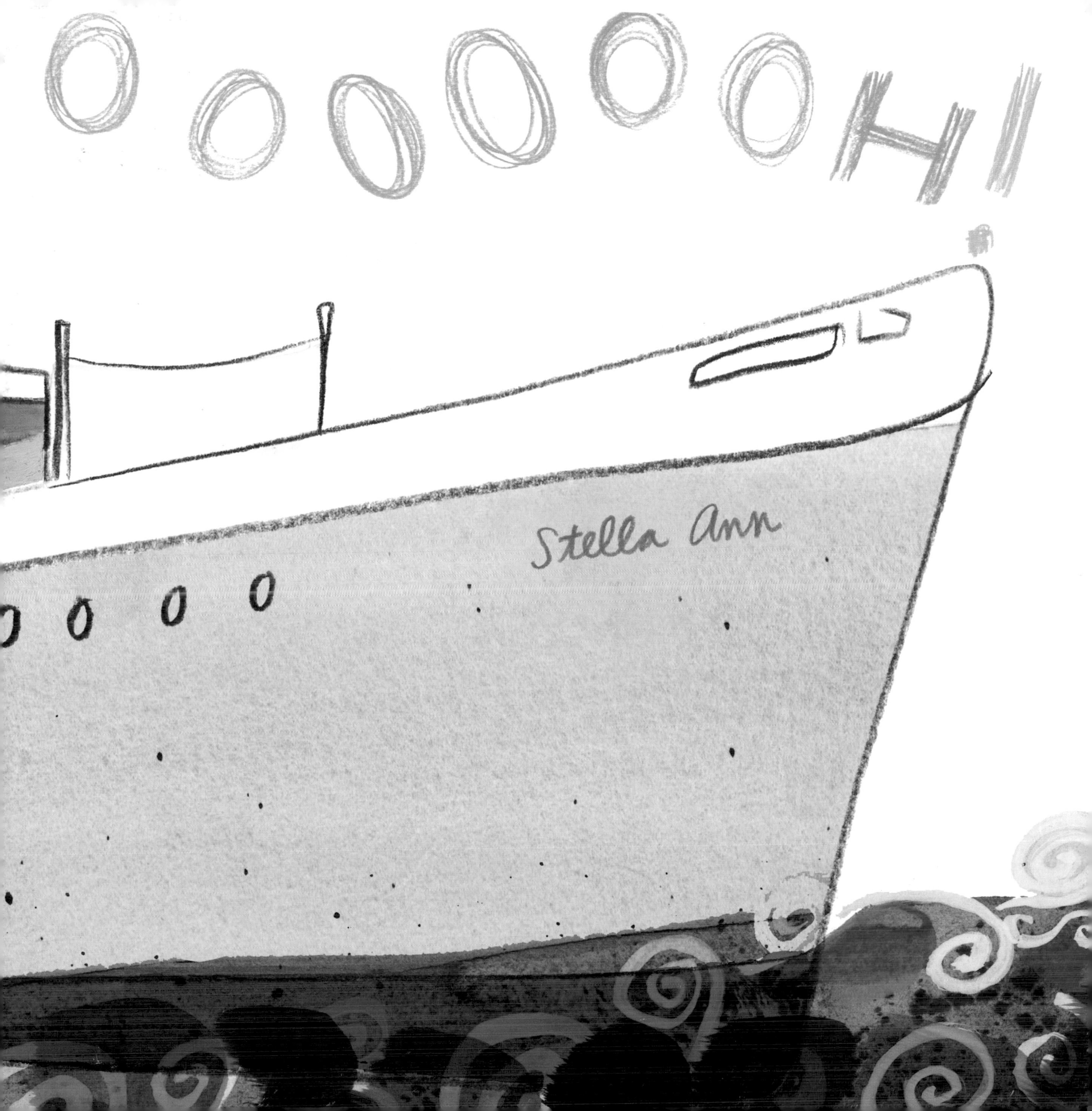
OOOOOOH!
Stella Ann

...and small ones.

shlurrp!

There were cheerful voices...

...and sad voices...

...even soulful, sniffly voices.

It seemed that everything in the world
had its own voice. Except Harold.

I **MUST** have my own voice, he thought.
It's got to be in there *somewhere*.

It's now or never, he decided.
He took a deep breath, and...

WHAT was THAT?!?

What a HORRIBLE noise!

But then something wonderful happened.

'What a GREAT voice!'
squawked the other parrots.
"We heard you from MILES away!"

That afternoon, Harold's new friends
listened to all the voices he could make.
They wanted to hear more, and more, and more...

When it was time for dinner,
Harold invited them back home.

Harold taught his friends to make all the voices
from apartment 4B. Of course, Harold was still the *best*
alarm clock. He made the *best* kettle noise. He was easily
the *best* washing machine. And he was the *best* shower!

But his own voice made him happiest of all!